D1473572

Snipp, Snapp, Snurr
and the
REINDEER

MAJ LINDMAN

ALBERT WHITMAN & COMPANY
Morton Grove, Illinois

The Snipp, Snapp, Snurr Books
Snipp, Snapp, Snurr and the Buttered Bread
Snipp, Snapp, Snurr and the Gingerbread
Snipp, Snapp, Snurr and the Red Shoes
Snipp, Snapp, Snurr and the Reindeer
Snipp, Snapp, Snurr and the Yellow Sled
Snipp, Snapp, Snurr Learn to Swim

The Flicka, Ricka, Dicka Books
Flicka, Ricka, Dicka and the Big Red Hen
Flicka, Ricka, Dicka and the Little Dog
Flicka, Ricka, Dicka and the New Dotted Dresses
Flicka, Ricka, Dicka and the Three Kittens
Flicka, Ricka, Dicka and Their New Friend
Flicka, Ricka, Dicka Bake a Cake

Library of Congress Cataloging-in-Publication Data
Lindman, Maj.
Snipp, Snapp, Snurr and the reindeer / by Maj Lindman.
p.   cm.
Summary: The three little Swedish brothers spend their
vacation in Lapland where they ski, visit a village of
Laplanders, and almost get lost in the snow.
ISBN 0-8075-7497-X (pbk)
[1. Skis and skiing—Fiction. 2. Snow—Fiction.
3. Brothers—Fiction. 4. Triplets—Fiction.
5. Lapland—Fiction.] I. Title.
PZ7.L659Snr 1995   95-1048
[E]—dc20   CIP
                                          AC

The text is set in 23' Futura Book
and 12' Bookman Light Italic.

A Snipp, Snapp, Snurr Book

They all put on skis and walked across the snow.

It was spring vacation time. Snipp, Snapp, and Snurr, three little boys who lived in Sweden, were very happy.

Father and Mother were going with them on a trip to Lapland.

They took a train and went to the mountains far in the north. They rode as far as the train could take them.

"We must go the rest of the way on skis," said Father.

They all put on skis and walked across the snow. Father pulled a sled with all their clothes and food on it. Mother walked behind, watching the boys. Their skis made tracks in the snow.

Just as Snipp, Snapp, and Snurr felt they could go no farther, they came to a little house at the top of a hill.

"This is where we are going to stay," said Father.

The snow-covered hills lay all around the house. Dwarf birches grew nearby.

"This is the only kind of tree that grows this far north," said Mother.

"We can start from those trees and ski down the hill," said Snapp.

Snurr's skis ran into one another. He fell flat in the snow. "Snow is better on the hill than in my face!" he said.

The boys laughed. Snurr knocked the snow off his red hat. He tried again.

"Snow is better on the hill than in my face!"

Every day the boys practiced skiing down the hill. They practiced until they could easily go down the hill on their skis without falling.

"You ski very well," Father said one day. "We can go on a ski trip now."

Snipp, Snapp, and Snurr followed Father across the snow.

When they had gone over some hills they saw some Laplanders' tents not far away.

"Oh, Father, please, may we visit the Laplanders?" asked Snipp.

"Yes indeed," said Father.

They saw some Laplanders' tents not far away.

W hy do they live in tents?" asked Snurr.

"Tents are easy to carry on sleds," said Father. "Laplanders travel with their reindeer, and they carry their homes with them."

The Laplanders came out of their tents. They were happy to have visitors.

The Laplander boy was named Matti. He wore a bright blue jacket.

Matti's mother gave the boys a hot drink. She wore a long skirt and a bright apron.

Snapp patted Sampo, the dog.

Father talked to Matti's father about his herd of reindeer.

Matti's mother gave the boys a hot drink.

If you visit us again, you can play with my reindeer," said Matti. "His name is Prince."

"We've never known anyone who had a reindeer of his own," said Snipp.

Matti showed the boys how to catch a reindeer.

"Let's practice with Prince," said Snurr. They threw a rope around Prince's big horns. Prince liked this game. He pulled very hard on the rope, and the boys fell down in the snow.

"It's a good thing we like snow," said Snapp.

"We're always in it," said Snurr.

They threw a rope around Prince's big horns.

The boys came to visit every day. Snipp, Snapp, and Snurr learned to play many games in the snow. They made snowmen. They made tracks with their skis.

The snow game which the boys liked best was hide-and-seek. Sampo liked this game, too. The boys hid behind a little snow hill, and Sampo looked for them. When the big dog found the boys, he barked and licked their faces.

Sampo liked the boys almost as much as they liked him. He seemed sorry each evening when Snipp, Snapp, and Snurr left.

On the last day of their vacation, Father brought the boys to say goodbye to their Lapland friends.

The boys hid behind a little snow hill.

I must go back right away to help Mother pack," said Father. "I will leave you here. But remember to start home well before dark so that you can follow my tracks."

"We will," the boys answered.

Matti's father sat with the boys in his little tent and told them many stories.

"In the far north," he said, "the sun never sets in the summer."

"How do you know when you should go to sleep?" asked Snapp.

"We go to sleep when we get tired," the Laplander said.

Matti's father told the boys about bear hunts and about snowstorms. "Sometimes people get lost in the snow and are never found."

Matti's father told the boys about bear hunts.

We must go home before dark, or we might get lost, too," said Snipp.

The boys looked out of the tent and saw that it was still light.

"Goodbye. Thank you," they said.

The boys put on their skis. They started home across the snow.

Suddenly a big snowstorm began. It blew in their faces. Snow covered the tracks Father's skis had made.

Snipp, Snapp, and Snurr could not see where they were going. They became very tired, but they walked on and on in the cold snow.

Snurr's skis came off, and he fell. This time he did not laugh at the snow in his face.

The boys could not see where they were going.

Snurr sat down in the cold snow and cried. Snapp sat in the snow, too. He was very tired.

"We are lost!" said Snurr. "And we can't get home."

The boys were frightened.

"Don't stay there!" shouted Snipp. "We have to keep moving or we'll freeze!"

He pulled Snurr up.

Snurr wanted to be brave. He stopped crying and wiped his eyes.

Snapp stood up, too.

But just as Snurr got on his feet, he was pushed down again!

This time he *did* laugh. Snipp and Snapp laughed, too. A big dog stood over Snurr, licking his face.

"We have to keep moving or we'll freeze!"

Sampo!" said Snipp. "Where did you come from?"

Snapp saw another animal. It was Prince, pulling a little sled.

Matti was riding on the sled. He waved at the boys and called loudly, "Hi there!"

"How did you find us?" asked Snipp.

"Sampo followed you and found you with his good nose," said Matti, "and Prince brought me here."

The three boys got in the sled.

Matti put some warm deerskins over them. They settled down in the sled. They were very happy to be on their way home to Father and Mother.

"Sampo followed you and found you with his good nose."

Mother and Father were standing in the door.

"We have been very worried," said Mother. She kissed each of the boys.

"We got lost in the big snowstorm," said Snipp.

"It was very cold and lonely," said Snapp.

"But our Lapland friends found us. They brought us home safely," said Snurr, hugging Sampo.

"Come in and get warm at the fire," Mother said to Matti.

"We have been very worried," said Mother.

Before the open fire the boys had a fine meal of sausages and roasted apples.

Sampo had two big sausages of his own.

Mother emptied all her oatmeal and cornflakes into a pail for Prince. Prince, who ate only reindeer moss every day, had the feast of his life.

At last, it was time for Matti to leave. Mother had tears in her eyes as she said goodbye.

"Thank you, Matti. Thank you, Sampo and Prince," said Mother. "Thank you for my little boys."

"Can you find your way home in the dark?" asked Father.

"Oh yes," said Matti, laughing, "Prince and Sampo can find the way."

Sampo had two big sausages of his own.

Central Childrens

JAN   2006